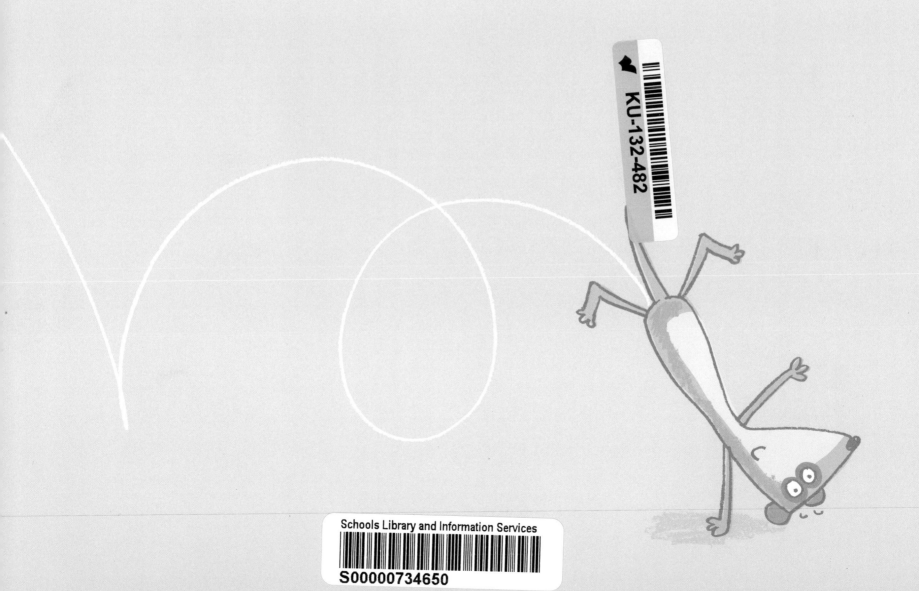

THIS WAY UP

AIR
MAIL

For Phil, Lori and Jamie.

SIMON AND SCHUSTER
First published in Great Britain in 2011 by Simon and Schuster UK Ltd, 1st Floor, 222 Gray's Inn Road, London, WC1X 8HB.

A CBS Company.

A CIP catalogue record for this book is available from the British Library upon request.

ISBN: 978-1-84738-578-9 (HB)
ISBN: 978-1-84738-579-6 (PB)
Printed in China

10 9 8 7 6 5 4 3 2 1

Millicent
and
MEER

Richard Byrne

SIMON AND SCHUSTER
London   New York   Sydney

One Saturday, Millicent was busy
making sandcastles in the garden

when . . .

THUMP!

A **big** wooden box landed beside her.

"Ouch!" said the big wooden box.

Millicent peeped under the lid.

A dazed-looking **creature** sat inside.

"Hello in there.
Are you OK?"
asked Millicent.

"Hmm, I think so," replied the creature, rubbing its head. "But I've got no idea who I am or how I got here."

Millicent giggled.
"You're **funny.**
Perhaps I can help?"

Millicent spotted a label on the big wooden box.

"Mm . . . ee . . . er . . . ka . . . t.

Mystery solved!" said Millicent.
"You're a cat and your name is Meer.

Yippee!

I've always wanted a cat. You can be MY cat."

She took Meer indoors.

Millicent **loved** her new cat . . .

. . . but he did do some
very **uncatty** things.

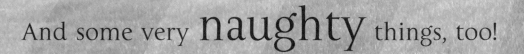

And some very naughty things, too!

Millicent's dad got **crosser** and **crosser**.

"RIGHT, THAT'S IT!" he said.
"Meer will have to go outside until he can learn
to behave like a **proper** cat."

Millicent didn't like putting Meer outside.

And Meer certainly didn't like **being** outside.

Poor Meer had been sitting all alone for some time when a stray cat came strolling past.

"Hey, why the sad face?" he asked.

"I have to stay outside until I can learn to behave like a **proper** cat," Meer explained.

"**Well**, old chap, you don't look like much of a cat to me but today's your lucky day. **Marvin's** the name and being a cat is my game. Just follow me."

Being a **proper** cat was a little tricky at first.

But Meer soon got the hang of it.

Then . . .

WOOF! WOOF!

"Dog! Quick! Run!" cried Marvin.

Meer wasn't sure what a dog was but he was sure that he didn't want to find out!

Marvin and Meer ran and ran until . . .

. . . something caught Meer's eye.

"Nice move, Meer," said Marvin. "We've lost him.
Now that was clever, even if you're NOT a cat."

"I'm not a cat?" replied Meer.

"No, look, you're a MEERkat!"

Marvin and Meer showed Millicent what they had discovered.

"So Meer isn't a cat doing **naughty** things. He's just a meerkat doing **meerkat** things," said Millicent.

"That explains everything," said Dad. "But it's not fair to keep Meer here. He belongs at the safari park with the rest of his family."

Later that day, a van arrived to take Meer back to his family.
Millicent and Marvin waved goodbye.

They were **really** going to miss Meer.

"Are you going home to your family too, Marvin?" asked Millicent.
"I don't have a home . . . **or** a family," sighed Marvin, sadly.

"Yippee!" said Millicent.

"I've always wanted a cat. YOU can be my cat!"

She took Marvin indoors.

Millicent and Marvin did lots of **fun** things together.

Millicent loved her new pet.
And Marvin loved his new home.

But, **best of all**, every weekend they went to the safari park and did lots of **meerkat** things with Meer and his family!

THE END